LOVE

MICHAEL S. A. GRAZIANO

Leapfrog Press
New York and London

Love

9 8 7 6 5 4 3 2 1
First published in the United States by Leapfrog Press, 2026

Leapfrog Press Inc.
www.leapfrogpress.com

Cover and text design: James Shannon and Prepress Plus, India

The cover image is a detail from: Salvador Dali *Inventions of the Monsters.* © 2026 Salvador Dalí, Fundació Gala-Salvador Dalí, Artists Rights Society

ISBN: 978-1-935248-378 (Paperback)

We make every effort to make sure our products are safe for the purpose for which they are intended. For more information see our website or contact our EU Authorised Representative, EAS Project OU, Mustamäe tee 50, 10621,Tallinn, Estonia, gpsr. requests@easproject.com

PRAISE FOR MICHAEL S. A. GRAZIANO'S FICTION

FOR *The Divine Farce*

"A Dante/Beckett reduction of human struggle to its lowest common denominator."— Michael Mirolla, author of *The Formal Logic of Emotion* and *Berlin*

"One of the most original and thought-provoking stories I have ever read... true literary art.... Not a word is wasted in this masterpiece. I have read many classics, and *The Divine Farce* should be counted among them; the finest in American literature."— *Geekscribe*

"Should be required reading in the writing grad schools.... There's nary a word wasted. What's left is comedy, retrospection, betrayal, tenderness, meditations on loneliness, a love story that survives all attempts to suppress it... not bad within 149 pages."— *Barnstable Patriot*

FOR *The Love Song of Monkey*

"Neuroscientist and author Graziano has crafted a compelling fantasy based on a semi-plausible "what if." Imaginative, intelligent narrative.... Twin ideas of forgiveness and mercy twist through this strange, moving, patiently wrought novel, making for a trippy but charming read."
— *Publishers Weekly*

"An hilarious, dark, brittle take on post-modern medicine, love triangles, the dense emptiness of contemporary life, and the power of contemplative self-discovery. Part magic realism, part science fiction, part theater of the absurd, and part over-the-top, unrepentant spoof, this novel packs more into its few short pages than do most epic trilogies. Perfectly woven, self-enclosed, multifaceted...Kosinski's *Being There* sprinkled with a strong dose of *Frankenstein*...the kind of simplicity that speaks volumes."
— *Michael Mirolla,* author of *The Formal Logic of Emotion*

"An amalgam of fairy tale, satire, science fiction, medical thriller, and soap opera. . . . It is difficult to fathom that a novel so brief can be so epic in scope. Inventive and deftly crafted."— Eric Linder, Yellow Umbrella Books, Chatham, Massachusetts

FOR *Death My Own Way*

"Darkly inventive. . . . Graziano's grim allegory interrogates human existence with its visceral, sensuous description."— *Publishers Weekly*

"A uniquely human story that proves humorous as well as thoughtful. Solid and very highly recommended." — *Midwest Book Review*

Chapter I

I am that caterpillar who is so enamored of his own cocoon that he won't come out. He won't metamorphose. Other caterpillars want flight – they *aspire* to flight – but me, I don't need it. I don't like change. The thought of actually wriggling out of my cocoon into the light is horrible to me. You already fly, so why should I? You are my wings. When you rip yourself away from me for days at a time, my body is left with a pair of ragged nubs where the wings used to connect, the pain is horrible, I want you back, but at the same time I enjoy the thought of your adventures, I enjoy vicarious loops through the meadow, this entomological fable is getting weirder every second. You've suggested that, while you're away, I should fill in the emptiness with somebody else – a secondary lover. I should be pragmatic, but the suggestion is sickening. I can't. I can't be physically close to, I can't make contact with, anyone other than you, not even casually, not even touching a person's hand, not without a subtle underdrag of nausea. Strangers touch all the time. You claim to enjoy the power trip of crushing a business competitor's paw. But me, I dread a handshake. My palm skin-to-skin against the moist palm of a stranger? Yech. I prefer the dry promise of my sketch pad. Friends hug each other, sometimes even peck each other on the cheek, but I can't do it. It's a loathsome image, a person's face looming at me like a giant piece of rotten fruit. Some people like to go all the way, take a sweat bath in bed with a stranger, as a regular hobby. Don't scowl at me. I'm not judging you. I'm not knocking anyone's lifestyle. I'm not a prude. I'm not a moralist. I'm merely explaining the way I feel. I have only one pair of wings, and you are my wings. You leave on one of your business trips, five days here, ten days there, and then come back to me. With a deft movement, you knit closed the rent in our chrysalis and we're sealed together again in the warmth and the darkness, the wings crumpling up against me. In a perverse way, I gain as much value out of the trip as you do. No, more. I insist. I spend the week anticipating your return, and anticipation is a gift. Nothing in this life feels better than the moment you walk in the door in the middle of the night. Whatever perfumes you may have picked up across the meadow, whatever scraps of other people's moods and personalities, lift my imagination. You are the *Hey are you awake?* (Whoa. That's unexpected. That's your voice. Your voice has a natural intensity, underlined *and* italicized, demanding my attention.) ~~What?~~ (That's my voice. I am the annotations put in and then, on further thought, with ambivalence, crossed out neatly but not erased, left legible in case I should later on find a useful meaning in the phrases.) Damn, how did she know I was still awake? Was I talking out loud? (That's my thought, the ordinary typeface of narrative, the matrix of my reality.) Did I accidentally blurt that chrysalis stuff out loud? I hate it when I accidentally talk drivel out loud and somebody overhears me. Sometimes I even *You're sniffing me. Do I smell?* I was sniffing out loud. Ha ha, good. I think that's acceptable. Now I'll *Do I smell like cigarette from that awful taxi? A little. Not too bad. Did I wake you up? I was quiet coming in. Thank you. No, I hadn't fallen asleep yet. I was pondering bug bodies and their wings (um, I'll explain later) and suddenly here you are.* All I see is darkness: the gray darkness of the ceiling, the many-colored darkness of the city glowing through the window drape, the black blob of the kitchen doorway that looks like a monster creeping up on our queen-sized bed. *I'm still on California time. Strange week. Strange trip. Hey, what are you, an octopus now?* You laugh as I hone closer to the heat of your body and wrap my limbs around you. *You're engulfing me in your tentacles. Are you trying to digest me? Yum. I love digesting you.* But the delightful conversation is imagination. Or anticipation. Your voice is spun out of the black and white of my own thoughts. You're not home yet. I'm always impatient when I expect you home. Home? I call it my home but the apartment really is yours. Seventeenth floor. You're the one with the high-flying finances. You should splurge a little on the interior decorating. The hideous window drape to my right is a nubbly reddish nylon material, like a bloody half-scraped animal hide or a used maxi pad, a fragment of the décor left over from a previous owner and never replaced out of sheer laziness. At night I like to pull it hard to block out the evening's artificial light. If I keep yanking on it, someday it's going to rip and we'll have to replace it. That's my hope anyway. Only a dim Manhattan glow seeps into the room. Through the drape, somehow, I can *sense* the presence of snowflakes hitting the outside of the windowpane the same way one senses people – the way one senses the presence of people in the next room over. I can sense the lightness and the quickness of those little snowy thought-creatures touching the window glass and disappearing with a silent laugh. I like that idea. Numerous beings of a primitive nature, a very short life span, and a monkish habit of silence, they fill up the urban space outside, crowding, drifting, jostling, outnumbering the humans eight trillion to one. In overcompensation for the snow and the cold outside, the room air is too hot and too dry. Must ask the building manager to adjust that. The radiator to the left of the bed gives off a dry heat and a faint smell of old cooked dust. It's a ribbed metal thing in white paint, gray in places, chipped down to the bare steel here and there. In the darkness it looks like a human ribcage humped beside me. The bed is framed by these two features of the room: the ugly sanguineous lumpy hide of a window drape to the right, and the skeleton of the radiator to the left. Very sepulchral. Very primeval. In Manhattan, a walk-in closet is a bedroom. And an apartment that consists entirely of a kitchen with a queen-sized bed crammed into the closet – that's halfway toward swanky. You, jetsetter, you could afford all-the-way-swanky, I am pretty sure. You could afford it, but what's the point? You're here a fifth of the time. A day in, a week out, three days here, eight days elsewhere. Butterfly wings. Occasionally, in all the haste, magazines and ice cream spoons fall down the crack between the bed and the wall and they are exceedingly hard to get back out. You ignore them, you don't care, they are details, you are off, you are out the door, but I've gotten bruises on my right arm especially around the elbow joint from wriggling it down that crack after lost items. Someday I'll pull up the mattress and do an archeological excavation. I wonder what detritus of your past life will be revealed? You see, don't you, how much I am fascinated by everything you? Even your dead skin cells. House dust, I once read, is mostly the dry outer layer of skin that we shed. You and I, our skin eternally together, intermingled in the grime behind the toilet, under the refrigerator and along the baseboards. It's romantic. Even when you're gone, when I'm gone, long after we're both dead and gone, we'll still be here, hidden in the cracks under the baseboard, slow-cooking. Tonight, the radiator next to the bed is working so hard against the winter that I'm being broiled in this little closet-oven. I kick down the sheets, careful not to let my feet touch the metal flanges of the radiator or I'll burn myself. I know from experience. I strip off my pajamas and toss them off the foot of the bed. They're sprawled somewhere on the fake-brick linoleum tiles of the kitchen. I'm lying stark naked on my back, legs together and crossed at the ankles, genitals hitched up so that they aren't squeezed between my thighs, stringy arms stretched to either side spanning the mattress, messy hair spread out over the pillow, like Christ before he was raised up vertically and planted in the ground. I don't think I have delusions of godhood – nobody has ever confessed a sin to me anyway – I simply find the spread-out Jesus posture comfortable. It flatters my limbs and the links of my spine. It liberates my mind. Aren't all artists really just perfectionists in the art of imperfection? I'm a perfectionist in the art of lying in a dirty bed, in a tiny, overheated closet-room, in an absent soulmate's apartment, in solitude, waiting for her return after a week of her opportunistic and probably unfaithful absence. Now *that* is perfectionism in the art of flaws. Quintessentially me. I don't even know if I'm bragging or self-mocking. Probably both. Look at me, I'm complete and incomplete. I'm complete because I possess something of extraordinary value. I possess a delicious longing. At the same time, I'm incomplete because I am, necessarily, without the object of my longing. If I had the object, I would no longer have the longing, and I would again be incomplete. It's an emotional incompleteness theorem. I'm longing for Achilles to return from the battle. Wheeling your black suitcase like your personal war chariot, shedding your buttoned-up armor of business attire, reeking of other people's cigarettes. You're due tonight sometime in the small hours, give or take the flight delay and the subway schedule. If the snowfall continues, you might not arrive until tomorrow, but I hope the flight is on time. The nickname Achilles, by the way, is a cubist metaphor, exposing several sides of you at the same time. The angry one? The one who fears her own mortality and therefore snatches at everything she can in a life of frenzied ambition? The killer of men? The woman with a perpetual Band-Aid on her heel because of a boot blister? I don't know. Supreme confidence in the cut of your suit, in the angle of your chin, in the leanness of your face, in the blackness of your tied-back hair. Maybe I flatter myself that my other half is half a god. And I do so admire you. Whatever this feeling inside me may be, this heat, this dread and longing, this love or rage, the contrary desire never to see you again and to taste every detail of your adventures, whatever the confusion in my heart, regardless of anything I may think or hope, eventually you'll come through the door kicking the snow off your shoes, knocking the snow off your knitted hat. Boom! I will shoot you in the head. No, no, that's in my imagination. I won't do that. You'll crawl into bed beside me and I'll wrap my arms and legs around you, and the intensity of the happiness will cause me pain. The intensity of the *need* is maybe more apt. One time, when you came home from a business trip in the middle of the night and I nuzzled my face against you, I noticed a faint but distinctly recognizable smell of orange juice lingering around your nipples. At first, I was puzzled – how odd is that? – but then I figured it out. Orange juice implies a hotel breakfast, maybe delivered by room service, followed by some indulgent morning sex, somebody's mouth on your breasts, then a glance at the clock, a sudden panicked realization about the time, a frenzy of activity, throw on clothes, no time for a shower, rush down to the lobby, catch a taxi to the airport – you see what a clever sleuth I can be? I admired how you didn't hide that telltale smell. It was what it was. It was a part of who you were at that moment and you were too exhausted to hide it and you never do hide anything, do you? I tucked my face against you. The odor, although not lovely in itself, added to the intensity of the moment. I had *you.* Not an imposter. Not a sanitized fantasy. The smell was proof of identity. I'm always grateful to have the real you because I know that someday you may never come back. One evening I'll expect you, I'll wait, I'll fall into confused dreams, I'll lose track of time in my half sleep, I'll wake up the next morning in the dry heat of the radiator instead of the moist living heat of your body, I'll wonder, I'll feel ill, I'll digest the inside lining of my stomach with an acidic worry, and in a week or so I'll find a legal notification slipped under the door to vacate the apartment because the owner, to wit,

Achilles, Slayer of Men, has hereby sold the property to a third party who will enter the premises on the X day of month Y and so on and so forth and this and that. And I'll be out of a home. Which, by itself, I don't mind. I've been homeless before. You rescued me from an acute bout of homelessness. I could stand it again well enough. It's not the home but the fire that I'd miss. You are self-immolation to me. I'm addicted to my anxiety about you, to the fear that you might never come back. If I were certain of you, if I were confident, if you were mine and no one else's, if you were merely at the supermarket buying a roast chicken and some Mac-n-Cheez for a cozy dinner in front of a pirated movie, if I felt around inside myself and missed that focused burning sensation of anxiety, maybe I'd run outside naked in the snow screaming, Help! Somebody help me! My pilot light went out! I'm going to die! If I were certain of you, what would I do with you? No, I need the uncertainty. Uncertainty is who I am. Artists have a high tolerance for it. We crave it. Art is killed by certainty. If I draw the clear and definite outline of your face with the tip of a well-sharpened pencil, I create a monstrosity. Something ugly with a toothy grimace, like the drawings that small-minded kindergarten teachers are at such pains to teach their children. A good drawing needs some obscurity to it, some smear, some shadow, some menace and chaos. It needs dirt. It needs *blood* smeared on the page. <u>*Draw me*</u>. How many times did you ask me that? How many times did I try? Each portrait satisfies me for a little while and then my understanding of you changes and the portrait no longer feels right. So I try again. You're aesthetically addictive. Consider this wordy rant to be the latest try at portraiture, my thoughts squirting out all directions in the double capacity of the paintbrush and the paint, splattering a picture of you across the ceiling, walls, nubbly red window drape, and too-hot radiator. No, but here's the problem: Truly, I can't draw you. I'm captive to my own perspective. I can only draw the you in the mind of the me who is familiar with the you who spends only a small amount of her time with the me who lives in this ugly apartment that I suspect is a dodgy tax write-off for you. Which means that I can't tell whether the picture I'm drawing reveals me or you, or just a kind of eggbeater blend of two fakes and who knows who is who. All the same, I'll draw the portrait. I'll start from the beginning of us on the first day that I ever saw you, and maybe that will straighten out the whos and the yous.

Chapter 2

Remember my old bench in Central Park? The one with the black-painted iron frame, hot to the touch in the sun? It has paint blisters, crumbling where the rust is coming through. The two, slightly warped oak planks that form the seat used to be varnished, but the varnish rubbed off a long time ago and now the wood is gray and grainy. I'm sitting at one end. Beside me, spread out on a white plastic CVS bag – my poor-man's version of a briefcase – I've arranged a box of cheap number 2 pencils, a sharpener, and pink erasers cut into acute angles with a pocketknife. In front of the bench, I've placed an old, battered aluminum-and-nylon beach chair, ocean blue. My customers sit in the chair enjoying the smell of the dry sun-baked soil, the smell of pencil shavings, of city air, of park lilies and late summer turning into early autumn. The people never quite look at me. They look at their laps, or over my head at the big maple tree behind me, at the yellow umbrella of the nearby peanut vendor, or they turn their heads offering me a degree of profile while they watch the roller-bladers on the black and white pebbly macadam path that curves beside the bench. They look everywhere and at everything except me. They're usually too embarrassed. I look homeless. Tattered jeans coming apart at the crotch. Denim jacket that was once green, but is mostly washed-out gray now, and is missing all its metal buttons. A T-shirt under the jacket, peeking through, old sweat-stained blue. My blond-brown hair hanging down greasy into the denim collar. I washed my face two weeks ago in a public bathroom. I do look the part of the starving artist. I don't intend to. I don't plan it as artifice. I simply am gaunt. My face is gaunt. My toes, sticking out from the broken ends of my sneakers, are skeleton toes. I sit with my pad on a plywood board on my blue-jean lap, my angles and elbows gathered over the pad. I sketch, they sit. I squint, they smile. I watch them closely and measure them, they pose. They smile and pose because they want to look good, and as a result, the first five minutes of the sketch are useless. Lifeless. Gradually the muscles of the face relax and then love can happen. Love, yes, love. Drawing a person's face is touching it, is touching something underneath the surface, something inside the person. I can love a man's eyebrow, its curve, the dip and meander that shades the meaning, that gives it slyness or sincerity. That man may think he's bored, he may sneak a glance at his watch and wonder how long he must sit in the buggy shade for his five-dollar sketch, but under that sun-dried leathery sheath of boredom is a psychological depth. The eyes are not the windows to the soul, for all that they attract one's attention. The eyes are easy. From the perspective of draftsmanship, they are blanks, simple teardrop shapes. They sit at the vertex and take on the meaning of everything surrounding them. They are collectors of meaning, re-transmitters of meaning, not producers of meaning, and it's everything else, everything gathering at the edge, that creates the expression. The eyebrow, the crow's-feet at the corner of the eye, the laziness of the eyelid, the tilt of the head, the line of the neck, the tension around the mouth, yes, especially that, but to me – and this is a truth that I've been a long time in realizing – the soul lies in the mobility of the cheeks. Human passion, human joy, lives in the upward bunching of the cheeks. I feel like I'm touching them softly with my fingertips, pushing them, like pushing soft clay on a sculpture, coaxing them, coaxing *soul* out of the face. My old school chums from another time in my life would have said, Dude, you're talking about a *guy*, loving a frickin' *guy*, dude, you know that? To which I say in my mind as my pencil is poised at the cheekbone, at the interface between shadow and the curling of the temple hair, Yes, yes, that's exactly right, a guy. Right now, a guy. In twenty minutes, a woman. In an hour, a very old man. In the afternoon, a child, a little girl, or a little boy, or a boy and a girl sitting together on the beach chair, posed by their parents, scowling in embarrassment while showing me their souls. And yes, in each of these cases I am talking about love. Drawing is an act of love that's contradictory because it puts a distance between you and the person you're drawing, turns you into a hire, lends you a clinical perspective, forces you to measure someone's face with your eye's micrometer, like an inspector measuring a factory product, and yet at the same time you find so much pure deep emotional attachment that it can be heartbreaking to give away the drawing. The drawing itself has a soul. It absorbs soul from the person, sucks it in, distills it, sends it back out again through the pupils. Didn't I already say so? The eyes are collectors and re-transmitters of soul, gathering it from the surrounding face and radiating it out of the page. And yet it's graphite smeared on paper. Nothing more. Sometimes barely that. A controlled smudge. I can't help wondering: For so little graphite, for so little actual *mileage* out of a pencil, how did the thing take as long as ten, fifteen minutes to produce? And how did it manage to steal some of the light of human consciousness? Well, well, maybe I love the drawing more than the person. *The* drawing, not *my* drawing. I don't love *my* drawing. As an artist, if you love yourself too much, if your ego eclipses the world around you, then you have no hope. Your work is contaminated. No, I love the thing sitting in my lap looking thoughtfully, meaningfully, out of the page at me. Ach, well, the drawing is as done as I can make it. I know that if I labor over it any longer, I'll only harm it, and so I must accept the heartache, I must tear it out of the notebook and exchange it for five bucks. The five bucks bothers me – mixing the profound with the mercenary. I'd give them all away for free if I could, one after the next, just for the drug of my version of love. But as skeletal as I am, as little as I eat, as gaunt as I look, as rarely as I change my clothes, as austere as I am in my renunciation of all things worldly, I do occasionally find it necessary to buy something. Picking free food out of the garbage bins behind the supermarket is chancy and bad for gastrointestinal health. As I have discovered. So I charge five dollars. I feel bad about it. I shouldn't charge the people who sit for me – after all, they're giving me the privilege, the thrill, of a new face to love. Instead, what I should do is charge the people who stand around and watch. I have no patience for voyeurs. They distract me from my drawing and they ought to pay a fine. Today a woman is standing behind me watching, resting her hand on the metal rail at the back of the bench. She says nothing; she hardly breathes out of an excess of respect; she simply watches the drawing unfold; and I ignore her; or try to. At first her presence intrudes. She casts a shadow on my mind. I've become so attuned to faces that the thought of one behind me pesters me. After a few moments, she dims in my consciousness, fades almost but not entirely, and I'm able to focus on the work. Three portraits, scratch, scratch, scratch, one after the next, it's a good morning. I don't often get a queue. When the second one is finished – a bearded man, a little man with a secret nervousness – "Thank you," he says, hunching forward in the beach chair, frowning over the picture, holding it by a corner, squinting in the sunlight that falls jittering through the maple leaves. I can see the emotion trembling at the corners of his mouth. He takes a quick breath and speaks his mind. His type is not so rare, if only he knew. A lot of people blurt out their thoughts on the spot. "It's terrible," he says. Then he shrugs. "I'm not a robber. Here's your five bucks. But . . . the hell am I supposed to do with this trash?" He gets up and walks away, still holding the drawing by one corner as you might hold a dead mole by the tail. I suspect he'll stuff it into a garbage can, though he'll probably wait until he's around the bend in the path. He flatters himself that he's honest but not cruel. The face that I drew has that personality, at least, and so I imagine the man must have it too. I fold up the five single-dollar bills, put them in a plastic sandwich bag with the rest of my money, and wriggle the bag into the front pocket of my jeans. The plastic protects the money from my sweat. Sometimes, as I concentrate on a drawing, I feel a bead of sweat growing on the tip of my nose and I make sure to wipe it away quickly on the back of my wrist. Nothing is more disruptive than a splash of sweat on my paper, spreading through the fibers like an infection. I used to have a rag for wiping sweat, a bit of an old shirt, but it became so grimy and smelly that it scared away the customers. The woman behind me, leaning a little over me to see the drawings unfold, must have a noseful of body odor. I'm still ignoring her. The next customer, the man now sitting in my chair, has a woeful face. A wonderful face. But don't they all? He's focused. He's thinking about something else. That scowl isn't anger; it's sheer concentration. He's sitting with extraordinary stillness, his hands loosely curled in his lap, as if the park around him has disappeared. I don't know what he's thinking about, and it hardly matters. The *way* he's thinking about it captures the essence of the man. He's so thoughtful – or thoughtlost – that when I'm done he looks at the drawing, looks for a long time squinting in the bright sun, seems to consider profound concepts, says nothing, does not even nod, simply looks, then pays, then stands, then leaves. No new takers at the moment. I unbend the angles of my arms and wrists and sit back, breathe the odor of the park, and am ready to eat lunch. An apple and a few slices of multi-grain bread. I try not to eat junk food. A candy bar can give me a buzz and a buzz ruins my focus. It prevents me from concentrating on my pencil. A soda is six times worse. I don't know why that woman is still standing behind me, silently, hand on the back of my bench, watching, spying. Must she spy on my food? I can understand the drawings, but the food? Her presence is beginning to enrage me. It's disrespectful. It's intrusive. I grit my teeth and turn sharply, ready to glare, or stab the pencil into her hand if I have to, the bitch, but nobody is behind me. And I realize: I have no idea how long that woman was present. Maybe she lingered for an hour. Maybe she stayed for thirty seconds, watching me draw half an ear until her idle curiosity was satisfied, and then walked away. I must have been so focused on the sketch pad that I didn't hear her leave. In my brain, she remained. Her faux presence bore into my skull from behind. I'm smiling at myself as I stuff the slices of bread in my mouth. They are the end, the final three slices of a loaf I bought at 7-Eleven. I had some idea of making sandwiches, but didn't have the money to buy the fixings, and so over the past few days I've been eating the bread by itself.

Bland, but I don't mind. I shake the crumbs from the empty bag into my hand, carefully lick them up, making sure I waste as little as possible, and disappoint a sparrow hopping on the dry dirt nearby. In thinking about whether I've eaten enough, carefully assessing the state inside my body, I notice that I'm still annoyed. Not at that woman, but at her ghost. At her image that my brain projected into the space behind me. Who does she think she is? Who do I think she is? Who is she? I feel a need to draw her in order to understand. Some people talk to friends and therapists, some go to church and talk to angels and gods. I draw. I take out the sketch pad again and gather myself over it, working, brushing off a late-summer maple seed that has helicoptered down onto the paper. I'm working from memory, but I still have a vivid impression of her face. I sketch her standing behind me, glaring over my shoulder. The difficulty with the woman is her right hand, the hand that's not resting on the back of the bench. I don't have a clear image of where to put it. Tucked in the pocket of her slacks doesn't work. Too "whatever" casual.

Both hands gripping the back of the bench? The pose makes her look too eager. Scratching at the side of her head looks too addled. But I solve the problem nicely. I give her a war spear. Her right hand is loosely curled around a wooden shaft, a shade taller than she is, topped by what appears to be a wrought iron point with scrolled barbs, made out of the same old black iron as the frame of the bench, a little bit rusted. I don't know what she's doing with that spear, but it feels right aesthetically. It suits her. It's a manifestation of her personality. She was poking that spear into the back of my brain for two hours. Jerk. The strange existential conundrum of the drawing grows on me. The woman standing behind the bench is a fantasy, a projection of the mind of the me in the picture. The me in the picture is just as much an act of imagination, a projection of the mind of the me who is sitting in the park drawing it. The me who is sitting in the park drawing is a memory and a projection generated by the mind of the me lying alone in bed, in Jesus posture, staring at shadows on the ceiling and waiting for you. The me in bed staring at the ceiling must be inside the imagination of some other me in some other place and time. Sometimes when the loops get too loopy, it's better to think less and focus more on the pencil. I finish the drawing of myself and the woman. I fill in a few blurry shapes of bushes at the edges and now I'm done. Looking up, looking around, judging by the feel of the crowd and the slant of the light through the gray city sky, I realize that I must have been more than an hour drawing her. The stiffness in my joints agrees. Pins and needles in my legs. I hope I haven't inadvertently turned away customers. Mommy, the mean artist man is ignoring us, let's just go away. I love the composition of the drawing. It fascinates me. Personality radiates from the page. I carefully use streaks of eraser to put beams of sunlight falling through it, falling over the bench, falling over the artist's lap, falling over the dusty ground, but despite the light, the mood of the picture is dark. A woman with a spear stands over a scrawny artist. I feel something predatory, something dreadful and seductive. I will keep this drawing. I'm glad I don't have to sell it. And I'm done drawing for the day. Sometimes I stay at my bench, pick up a new face and another five bucks every few hours, stop when the sunlight behind me begins to fail and the shadow of my head darkens up the page too much. But today, I'm done by three o'clock. My enigmatic drawing has left a residue in my mind, and I know from experience that an emotional residue will contaminate any further attempt at work. I close the picture into the notebook, careful not to smudge it, and put it away in my plastic shopping bag. Then I fold up my beach chair, hitch it over my shoulder, and walk away. I'm empty of mind in the sun in a crowd. Maybe that is happiness. Empty on a summer's day walking through the park in a crowd of faces that I don't need to deconstruct, that I don't need to draw – that I can ignore if I want to. Empty with the heat of the sun on my hair, my hair clinging tightly to the curve of my skull and swinging loose and long around my jaw with a rhythm that's heavy with sweat and natural oil, the familiar weight of the lawn chair's aluminum bar on my right shoulder, pressing lightly down on my clavicle, the familiar feel of the bag in my left hand, the plastic slippery with sweat against my fingers, the familiar weight of the supplies in my bag occasionally hitting my leg as I walk, a lean efficient walk, tendon and bone, tall, stretched, skinny legs, wire and metal, unbreakable, unstoppable, as if I've been wound up and my motor will go forever, the momentum and balance of my legs carrying me, the energy coming from inside me and around me and flowing naturally through me and propelling me forward, the gravel crunching under my sneakers, the soles of my sneakers worn so thin that I can feel the heat of the ground, feel the contours, feel the pebbles and the bumps, my feet gripping the earth, each step an act of seizing and possessing and then letting go and passing on, all the while I have no goal, simply walking the crowded paths, walking in the sunlight in the park. Title: Satisfied Homeless Guy Perambulating. Portraiture again. I'm addicted to it. Just like some people suffer from a sugar addiction. Or a sex addiction. Or a shopping addiction. Or a center-of-attention addiction. Or a money addiction. Or a power addiction. Which all sounds narcissistic to me. But I understand what it is to be addicted, because I am portrait addicted. Which is a misnomer. It's like saying that you're coffee cup addicted. You are, of course, addicted to the stuff inside the cup. So I am addicted to the feeling inside the portrait. I used to walk back and forth across the park and visit the art museums on the West and East sides. West Side one day, East Side the next. I can't now. I can't make it past the door wardens because my clothes are too sweaty and ragged, I smell too much, I look too homeless, and anyway I have nowhere to stash my beach chair and my plastic bag of supplies without risking another homeless person finding them and making off with them, which did happen to me once. I used to go to the Museum of Modern Art and stand in that moon-colony, air-conditioned breeze in front of a particular statue in a glass case. This favorite statue of mine was about two feet tall, brown polished wood, a dim light shining on it, a three-thousand-year-old carving of a woman with a water jug on her head. Egyptian. I don't know why it was in a museum of modern art, unless all of human civilization is considered to be modern by geological standards. I used to stand quietly and stare at that object. Egyptian art is usually stylized. It has more to do with Picasso than Vermeer. It has its beauty, elegance, skill, symbolic meaning. The line between art and pictogram is blurred. But here was something different. Here was an artist who had broken tradition with his peers and done something strictly realistic. I could see in this woman more than surface accuracy, more than detail. She was envisioned from the bones outward. She was biologically real. Her bones supported her muscle and fat and skin. Gravity pulled on her. The meat of her buttocks hung under her dress. A twenty-something woman behind me whispered to a friend, *Look, that person's a perv, staring at her boobs for an hour. Probably wants to hump her.* An explosion of suppressed giggles. Yes, yes, a perv. I suppose so. But also, no, I didn't actually want to touch the statue. And that was the point. It was so alive that it stirred my own peculiar revulsion toward the physicality of another human being. I haven't been back to see her in a few years. I don't need to

– she's in my head now. And the park is so full of inadvertent sculptures that I don't miss the inside of a museum. Every moment is a sculpture. Art is experience and experience is perpetual. I have my own Central Park Art Gallery and I enjoy an endless succession of paintings, such as: I am walking in the sun. I am walking beside the lake. I am squinting in the reflection from the lake. I am stooping over a water fountain. I am drinking rusty water. I am rinsing specks of multi-grain bread out of my mouth. I am wetting my palms to cool myself down. I am sitting on a rock in the sun. I am closing my eyes and waiting for the evening. I am picking my nose and putting the snot carefully on the rock beside me. I am considering whether I should buy myself dinner. I've made good money today. Yes, I can afford the indulgence of dinner, but I'll wait until after a nap. I deserve the nap. I've slept here and there in the city, but I've never slept on a rock before. I've tried sleeping in a doorway. In an alley behind a dumpster. Under bushes in the park. In tunnels. Culverts and access tunnels and storm drains and sewers. I don't like the tunnel system because too many people live in it. I don't like homeless shelters for the same reason – too crowded. I don't need shelters except in bad weather. Now in good, late-summer weather, in sunlight, in warmth, having everything I need, a satisfactory if unimaginative lunch in my stomach, a good day of work behind me, a purpose that defines me, a rock with a comfortable scoop fitted to my body, a shadow in my mind, a dissatisfaction, a worry, just present enough to provide a depth to the pleasure of the moment, since there can be no light without shadow, given that mix, given that perfection, how could I not? I allow myself to fall asleep, I allow the sleep to deepen and I allow myself to miss dinner. I sleep lazily through the afternoon and into the night. During the night I roll onto the grass next to the rock and smell the earth and the thin scrappy lawn, and wake up in the early morning to the changing gray-brown-green-blue brightness and the rising sound of traffic that surrounds the park. Who am I to want anything different from what I have? I don't care for achievement. My status is neither low nor high. I span levels and loops of thought and emotion, above and within and beneath all other people. It's a terribly lonesome life and sometimes nothing can be better. I don't want a house. I don't want a job. I don't want a clique of friends and associates. I don't want a serving of domesticity measured out by factory aliquot. I don't even want a name. I want to belong to everything and nothing. I'm a god after all, it seems. I am the universal observer. I am in my most natural, deistic, cruciform posture on the grass in Central Park, lying on my back with my legs together and crossed at the ankles, my genitals hitched up into the baggy crotch of my jeans so that they aren't squeezed between my thighs, my stringy arms stretched wide, my hands slightly curled, palms open to the sky, my greasy blond hair spread out on the ground, as if I own the world and am welcoming it, every aspect of it to a new day. Something inside me has opened during the night. Maybe one of those maple seeds helicoptered down into my innards and germinated? I'm expecting something to happen today, but I don't know what it might be. My intuition is whispering to me. My body is physically asking the world the most fundamental question – what's next for me? I don't mind not knowing the answer. Right now, the anticipation is enough.

Chapter 3

I sit up and brush bits of soil and grass from my clothes, then gather up my belongings and walk in the early morning, breathe the cold dawn air, send up faint wisps of breath, wander among the empty paths, finally sit on my bench under the maple tree in the new light, the beach chair opened and set at an enticing angle in case of business. The crowd starts early in Central Park. Six o'clock the joggers are out, sweats on, rubber-coated dumbbells in their fists, but they are rather purposeful folk and not potential customers. Usually my clientele arrives after ten o'clock, casual tourists in their own city. And yet here I am, set up at the break of dawn. I have a craving for discovery today, a feeling that something new will happen. And that's when you, *you*, you walk up the path, supremely confident, and sit on my beach chair, one leg crossed over the other. _Draw me_, you say. Your voice is authoritative. It demands attention. You are a ridiculous wasp-ish alpha businesswoman. Surely it's a farce that you've strutted into my moment and are masquerading as the answer to my fundamen-tal question – what's next for me? Really? You're next for me? I can't help grimacing, al-though I don't want to be rude to a customer. Who are you? I admit, on close examination in the morning light, that you look nothing as bad as I expected, nothing like a rich-bitch, plastic mannequin, posed in the window of a high-end clothing store. I can see some possi-bilities for a portrait in the width of your cheeks and the subtle furry connection between your black eyebrows. You have black hair and a white, heart-shaped face, with a widow's peak at the center of your forehead. You have an athletic build underneath the business suit, a hint of healthy cavewoman about you, espe-cially in the robust musculature of your legs, which are bulging in your business slacks, sug-gesting to me a previous career in collegiate track and field. I open my sketch pad, lift out my drawing from yesterday, and hand it to you. The gesture annoys you. You want me to draw a portrait of you, not hand over a canned sketch. You pull back your head with a frown that says, _Hey, Service Boy, you think I came here for a joke? I pay. You hop._ Then you glance down at the drawing, see what it is, and begin to laugh – a deep spasm of a laugh. I've surprised you. _I thought you hadn't noticed me yesterday._ ~~I'm an artist. It's my job to notice people.~~ _I'm flattered but . . . you drew me with a spear._ I respond with a bland smile and a shrug at your perfectly accurate observation. Studying the portrait, you say, _I don't know if it's a compliment or an insult._ ~~I never draw insults. Not intentionally, anyway. I only ever draw what I see.~~ _You never get the urge to draw an unflattering revenge portrait?_ ~~Never.~~ _You're very patient, given the insults that you get from your customers. What did that man call your work? Dreck? Trash?_ You hand the picture back to me and I put it away safely between two pages. Your look is intent. One eye is closed and the other eye squints at me against the bright morning light. The sun-contracted prick of your pupil is your spear point. I see you more and more clearly. I see your face. I see your confidence. I see the forward tilt of your head. I see your black hair with a hint of rainbow iridescence from the sunlight. I see money in your posture. I see ego. I see intelligence. I see the whiteness of your hands folded in your lap. I see five perfect manicured nails on your right hand and five chewed edges on your left. _That drawing,_ you tell me with some exasperation in your voice, _is art. It's gallery value. You know it. Nobody is that good and doesn't know it. What are you doing, selling your art for five dollars apiece as if it's kitsch? To people who don't appreciate it? You could get four figures for it, if you knew where to sell it._ You sound disgusted, as though I'm intentionally committing the sin of financial devaluation. I'm an agent of economic mayhem, I guess. A subversive. I like that! I take out my pencil, sharpen it, rub the point between my fingertips to get off the burrs, prepare my plywood board and my paper for another sketch. ~~Would you feel better if I drew bad portraits, instead of gallery value?~~ You roll your eyes, spread your hands, expel an _Uhhh_. Fool of an artist. That's what you're thinking. And now I see that you see me. You see me. You know that what I see is essence. Not value. I care nothing about financial value. All I want is to draw. But you, you see value. You care nothing about artistic essence unless it's got market value. That would seem to make us opposites, except that it doesn't. It makes us the same. My ability to see and capture essence *is* my market value. And your ability to trade in value *is* your essence. So we understand each other perfectly, and are both connoisseurs, each in our own way. You're the first customer to sit in my chair, look directly back at me, and understand me in the same way that I understand you. Your eyes are calipers as much as mine. To be seen at all is a novelty to me. Squinting, I take a try, sketch two, three, ten lines in ten seconds, and then hand you my new effort, a potato head with a snarl and a dollar sign hidden in the hair. It makes you laugh again. *Oh, Starving Artist. You're such a wag. I heard about you – I heard a rumor and had to come see for myself. I'm here to make a business proposition. And to get my portrait drawn. For real – not like this. And, by the way, I*

HATE potatoes. I hate everything to do with them. I have a trauma response to potatoes. You roll your eyes at my drawing and the gesture looks reflexive, like a tic. Then you grin. You're chronically outraged and chronically amused. You're appraising me again, my leanness, the translucency of skin in the hollow part of my temples, my lanky hair flowing into my collar, my jacket with the brass buttons missing – I see your eyes traveling down the length of me to the shredded cuffs of my jeans and my ripped sneakers. The CEO and the homeless. The faint odor of a tasteful perfume and the reek of park fart and sweat. Behold this study in contrasts. We're walking through the park together, my plastic bag dangling from my hand and my beach chair, mine, my chair, hooked over your shoulder, as if you own it. Why am I with you? Your business proposition repels me. Business is ugly, crabbed ink on paper. As for your contact, your "in" on the art world, the creature who runs an uptown art gallery, to whom you'd like to pass my drawings for his smarmy approval and marketing acumen, I have no interest in the dreadful, pretentious sophisticate, unless I can draw him too, and he will not like his portrait. I'm with you because I'm seduced by the drawing I made yesterday. That's what I tell myself, anyway. I want to see deeper into your personality than the partially reflective, dark glass, financial surface you're showing me this morning. The business wheeler and dealer. Yesterday I saw an honest spear woman, and I want to see more of her. I know something real must be hidden inside you, or you wouldn't have stopped to talk to me in the first place. You have a swagger about you, a relaxed stride, a physicality to the posture of your arm and hand as you hold my chair hooked over your shoulder. Primeval womanhood: strong, muscled, confident, successful. Modern manhood; thin, starved, twitchy, sensitive. I almost never leave the park, but now I am lured, I allow myself to be lured, into the crowded asphalt delta that spills onto Fifth Avenue. We reach the heat and the din of a mechanized civilization. I am not enamored of acoustic chaos. I'm not used to it. What keeps me with you now is the fact that you've got my customer chair and I don't want to lose the damn thing, otherwise I think I would bail. I tag behind you, hopping around the counter-flow of people. Traffic booms past. You're supremely indifferent to the noise. You stride at a New Yorker's pace underneath a rusty iron-and-lumber scaffold that runs the length of the block. I trot behind you. We reach the brass metal doors of an apartment building and enter the lobby. Sound and sight are dimmed in the shadows and the air is cool. I have not walked into a building, except the concrete bathroom bunkers in the park, and sometimes the subway tunnels, in, say, six months, eight months, long enough that the moment has an impact. You, you can have no idea what's going through my mind. How could anyone who lives in your world conceive of the sensory impact, the emotional impact, of walking through the front doors of a building? The gesture is mundane to you people. You don't even notice anymore. To me, it's an Event. The chaos disappears. The street sounds are gone. I've walked from one ecosystem directly into another – brass-grilled mailboxes mugging at me from one side, shabby elevator doors looming at me from the other, black-and-white checkered marble floor polished and yet slightly gritty from street dust, a smell of pine and bleach lingering from the last time the janitor mopped. A varnished wooden counter is set into the shadowed corner of the vestibule, and a guardsman sits behind the counter with an impressive police air about him as he texts on his phone. An austere silence. The lobby forms its own quiet, eternal peace. The security guard glances our way and his eyes casually meet yours. His expression shows boredom and familiarity. One ordinary glance and I can feel the hair rising on the back of my neck. He knows you and you know him. How do you two have such a casual familiarity? Obviously, you live here. If you live here, then we're not visiting your business contact, the curator of an art gallery, are we? We're visiting *you*. You've led me three blocks to invite me upstairs to your own home, or one of your homes, and I've only just realized it. Are you trying to kidnap me? Or seduce me? How incredibly stupid of me. Am I not a reader of faces? I should have known from the moment you framed your business proposition – from the moment you first sat down in front of me. The look in your eyes and the tilt of your shoulder should have tipped me off that something wasn't right, but the thought was too far from my mind. You're on a lark, a rich brat's adventure. Maybe it's a kinky dare? An adrenaline rush. I dare you to fuck that raggedy-ass Central Park artist, if you can. How did I miss such an obvious interpretation until this moment? I can't help a flicker of a smile at my own naiveté. I have to consider whether to accept the adventure, or to snatch my chair off your shoulder, run straight back out the lobby doors, and escape. Or am I reading too much into a passing look? Sometimes I lose the distinction between my own hair-trigger imagination and reality. Your body language shifts instantly, as though you've detected the tension in me. Maybe you're as sensitive to the world around you as I am. You lean closer to explain in a low voice, echoing in a whisper through the marble lobby, *I thought we could put your things down here and talk it over first. I don't use this apartment much, but it's in the neighborhood.* You gesture me into the elevator. *Have you had* _breakfast?_ I never eat breakfast. I lean back against the metal wall of the elevator, the vibration coming in through my shoulder blades and up through my feet, meeting in an uncomfortable jumble in my gut. I watch you as you watch me. I know I have poor social polish, a result of observing too much and participating too little and caring absolutely nothing about the effect I have on other people. I have an off-putting tendency to answer the actual question underneath the words. ~~Just so you know. I have trouble when people get into my personal space. I can't take it. Too much intensity comes in through the eyes, somehow.~~ You answer with a piercing look, a flick of your connected eyebrows and a hint of a grin. On the seventeenth floor, we walk down a long, hushed stretch of carpeted hall, dark red apartment doors to either side. You unlock a door and we step into an efficiency kitchen, a tiny room where you lean my folding chair against the refrigerator and I put my plastic bag down on the small Formica table. The apartment has a stale, closed-in odor. I can smell soap from the open bathroom door. I can smell rust from the faucet. I can smell old coffee. The wall is covered in yellow flowered wallpaper – an eyesore. As far as I can tell, the whole apartment is a kitchen. It's two chairs around a small round table. It's a walk-in space with adjoining closets. Dominating the wall, incongruously, hangs a large framed reproduction of a Dali, colorful and masterful and, psychologically at least, a hundred times larger than the apartment itself. The room is filled. The space is crowded by five personalities: you, me, my filthy folding chair leaning against the steel face of the fridge, my CVS bag of art supplies on the table settling with a crinkling, chattering sound, and Dali looming over us. We are convened here today (says the warning in my head) so that you can seduce the park portraitist. By closing the door behind us with my own hand, I think I've just given you permission. It's your game now, and I'm wondering how you'll go about playing it. We have nothing to hide from each other. You know that I know that you know. That kind of understanding is possible only between people who make a living out of measuring other people – unless I understand nothing, and it's all my own delusion. You pull open a drawer and take out a green terry-cloth kitchen towel. At first, I think you're going to wipe your hands after carrying my folding chair, an act of contempt or disgust, but nothing like that. Instead, with a mischievous grin, you dangle the towel in front of me by one corner. *What did you say? When people get too close, they get into your eyes and overwhelm your brain?* She wiggles the towel. *Is that supposed to be a blindfold?* I didn't expect so perverse a sense of humor, and I'm delighted. We can't help a mutual bark of laughter as I take the kitchen towel and tie it over my eyes. And you're right. The world does take a step back. The little kitchen expands around me and loses its tacky specificity. I feel calmer – like a parrot with a cloth over its head. Your voice now seems to come from all directions. It resonates. *You look stylish. But you still look nervous. What are you afraid of? My problem isn't fear. Then what is it? Overstimulation. My sensory nerves are thicker than the normal kind. I don't know. The world is like laser beams burning into me from all directions. I don't want a laser beam so strong that it burns me into a crispy pork rind. Does that make any sense? I watch, I draw, I'm non-participatory. That's who I always am.* You get loquacious when you can't see, don't you? I don't know. This is a new experience for me. *I'm sorry if I sound naïve, but why do you want to avoid burning up? Avoidance of self-immolation is, ipso facto, valid. It doesn't require syllogistic argument. Holy fuck, a philosopher. Ha! I had no idea you'd be so interesting. I thought we'd have a boring chitchat, a little business about your art, a little disappointment about your personality, and I'd throw you out. This is getting better every minute. Listen, never avoid the fire. An occasional, emotional self-immolation is good for you; it's a necessary aesthetic experience. If you don't let yourself feel, if you don't take risks, I don't think you can be an artist. What do you suppose Dali felt when he painted that picture? He didn't feel anything, because he didn't paint it. It's a cheap reproduction.* Your hand comes to rest lightly on the center of my breastbone where the last button of my denim jacket ripped out a few days ago. Your closeness to me is overwhelming. Even though your touch is light, I can still feel the enormous weight of your confidence behind it. I am in a crispy-pork-rind moment. *For your information, and between you and me, my philosophical friend, it isn't a reproduction. It's an original.* I'm sure you're lying. The proposition is ridiculous. An original Dali would cost millions and wouldn't be squirreled away in so unlikely and hideously ugly a mustard-yellow setting. At least, I hope it wouldn't. But the idea is so gorgeous that I want it to be true. Are you really that casually rich? Are you a compulsive owner? A high-end hoarder? Are you Gatsby acquiring your own park artist to store in your own Manhattan apartment along with your own Dali? Is that what this is all about? Acquisition? I feel light-headed. The pressure of your hand on my breastbone increases ever so slightly and gives me a steady point of reference. *Don't fall over, Starving Artist.* You lead me to a seat, which, I notice, is not a kitchen chair, but something soft – the edge of a bed. By the time the knot at the back of the blindfold shakes open and the visual world takes form around me again, we're lying together on a jumble of blankets in a dim, low-ceilinged closet. A boney radiator looms to one side and a blood-colored drape covers the window on the opposite wall. The morning sunlight struggles through the fabric and casts a pink tint through the alcove. We're in a coffin. We're in a tanning bed. A cave. A lean-to. A vagina. A gazebo. A shower stall. An asshole. An eggroll. A copper bullet casing. A chrysalis. A length of sewer pipe. An iron maiden. A ketchup bottle. An old plastic soda bottle stuck in the mud. Art images pop into my mind in a counterrhythm to our undulations. I think my brain is trying to detach itself from the moment. We are naked, we are efficient, we are done. We take a rest beside each other in the morning warmth, your nose squashed against my boney shoulder. Of all the thoughts that could float through my mind in this state of bewildered post-coital exhaustion, here is what I'm thinking: You never asked me to take a shower. I'm a homeless dude. I haven't changed my clothes in three months. Yeah, I'm an artist. I flatter myself that I'm a park icon and I even look a little like a doe-eyed Jesus, but I'm still homeless and I know that I stink. I mean, do you have a raunch fetish? Who knows what diseases you might catch on a gritty adventure with an indigent person. I can't help blurting out the question unfiltered: ~~*How can you stand the smell?*~~ Your voice leaks out indistinctly against my shoulder. _Oh, but the smell is so primal male, really._ Those words declare us to be archetypes. Primal male and primal female. Two people at the end of the simplest story of all. We meet, we fuck. One morning in the park, you sit down in business formal and ask me to draw a portrait of you. Twenty-three and a half minutes later, my sperm is inside you. Don't you find something archetypal and yet strange about that transaction?

Chapter 4

It won't be a one-off. I'm sure of it. After all, you have a financial interest in my drawings and the samples are going to take me months to produce. Sitting in the park sketching for a day, two days, three days after our first morning together, I'm expecting you to show up again. The matter is scrubbed of all suspense. It isn't a romantic fantasy; it's transactional reality. I'm not sure I want the taint of a business transaction contaminating my art, but the connection between us has sprung into existence regardless, and now as I'm waiting, waiting for you to show up again, look what you've done to me. I was God. I was myself. I was alone. I was artist and hermit and enlightened Buddha. I was truth. I was self-constructed and self-contained. Now I'm just another dude waiting for his date. Damn. I'd rather love everyone at a distance through my art than try to love one person up close and fail at it, like as not. Is that the lesson you've been put here to teach me? Deflating self-insight? On the third day, late morning, you pay me a visit. You sit on the bench beside me, brown paper napkin spread neatly on your lap. You're eating a croissant sandwich with a thin slice of ham and melted cheese. I refuse your polite offer. I don't eat breakfast. The calories cloud my mind. They make me sleepy. The artist in me is enraged by your presence. I'm working. I'm drawing. I'm focusing on my pad. My eyes are caressing the face of the person in front of me while your odors are trickling over me. Canadian bacon and melted Swiss on a buttery croissant, a mocha whiff from a cardboard cup, the chemical smell of dry-cleaned business formal, the apricot tint of shampoo, and something else, a solvent just under the surface of detection, a vapor that exhales from the pores of your skin. You eat. Brush crumbs off your lap. Scratch the tip of your nose. Distract me. What bothers me most, however, is that I'm not sufficiently bothered. Your smells enter the portrait that I'm drawing and fuse with the man's personality. He's not only shy, and self-doubting, and brittle at the arch of his eyebrow, but he's also subtly Canadian bacon and Swiss, shampoo and solvent and you. What are you doing to me? I'm already stirring your pigment into the graphite. The youness smooths the granularity. You're gone for a week and then show up again as though no time has passed. Then gone for three weeks, no sight, no sound, no smell of you, then back again. After that long vacation, somehow we're old pals. Every few days, you come by. Often we say nothing to each other. You relax beside me, you watch me draw for half an hour, you sip your coffee, you seem to absorb something satisfying from the fact that I can tolerate you. I don't know what experiences you might have suffered in your past, or might suffer every day in your current dog-eat-dog world of finance, to make so mundane a thing as a man's tolerance valuable to you. Especially a man so low down on the social totem pole as me. Sometimes, after your coffee, having satisfied whatever need you had by sitting quietly next to me as I sketch, you get up and stroll away, and I don't see you again for several days. Sometimes, when my customers run thin, we take a walk together, visit Dali, fuck. You don't appear to use the apartment for any other purpose. The bed sheets are always in the same twisted pile from the last time, weeks earlier. Afterward, we stroll back to my bench. A balding Wall Street gent sees us walking together and stops abruptly, staring, slightly bug-eyed, his mouth open, his briefcase oscillating in his hand. He doesn't even look at me – I seem to be invisible to him. He glares at you. The sight of you with a homeless person must have fried his brain. You're perfectly calm. You smile. *Don't you know the Central Park artist? You can get your portrait drawn, if you like.* The man shakes his head in outraged confusion and then flumps away. You shrug and sip your Starbucks, then pause as if considering the taste. *I used to date that guy, but I can't stand him anymore.* Your voice is pleasant, as if you're enjoying the diversity of a world in which people are free to be jerks – and I'm beginning to admire you. We reach my bench and I set up for my afternoon customers, but you don't leave yet. _Actually, Starving Artist, I've been meaning to give you something, in case it rains out here and you need a place to sleep . . . or to keep your notebook dry . . . ._ You hand me a brass door key and I put it in the front pocket of my denim jacket. You don't quite make eye contact. I think the generosity embarrasses us both. You drain the last of your coffee, crumple the cup into a nearby garbage can, and leave. The key is a little weighted marvel in my pocket. A warmth spreads from it into my heart. I wonder if the gift is partly a reaction to that elitist Wall Street creep – maybe it's your way of proving that for every act of jerk, there's also an act of generosity. I visit the Dali apartment later that day. The lobby guard recognizes me and lets me pass with his usual bored glance, I let myself into the apartment, and its emptiness goes so far up the scale of delicious that I feel guilty. You're not here, nobody's here, the city is muffled, the street is far below me through a dirty window above the kitchen sink, nobody is looking my way, no eyes are on me, heck, no eyes are intentionally avoiding me either. I've disappeared from the world. The silence makes the tiny space immense. The sink in the bathroom drips like the sound of stalactites in the depths of a cave. I sit at the little circular kitchen table, spread out my pad and my drawing tools, and sketch from memory. In this private space, I can absorb myself in the drawing. I can reach a mental peace impossible when I'm outside surrounded by a noisy reality. Are people allowed to disappear inside themselves so entirely? Did you mean to give me a sheltered place to spin my own cocoon? Did you know? I doubt it. I can't bring myself to sleep the night in this degree of silence, especially since it's filled up with an afterimage of you. I feel like I'll lose myself in it if I stay. I leave the drawing on the table for you to find. It shows a metal mesh garbage can, the kind dotted all over Central Park. This one is under a lamppost, and it's empty except for a single, crumpled-up piece of paper – which, secretly, is supposed to represent one of my own drawings that somebody threw in the trash. I don't know why that image is in my mind right now, but I like the way the light falls on the mesh. I like the broken-up shadow on the concrete ground. I don't know what you'll think when you find it. Something profound, to sell to your art-dealer friend? To be honest, I don't think it means anything. I just like the way it looks. And drawing my own discarded work amuses me. I like the irony and the self-deprecation. Whether you appreciate it or find it underwhelming as the first install-ment in the art series I'm giving you, I don't think it will put you off me. It seems you've made the calculation and decided to acquire me. You've rubber-banded us together the same way I rubber-band my pencils for safe-keeping. Our mutual loop of elastic is roomy and has a slow resonant frequency. We find a rhythm, toward and away, every four or five days, a week at the most. Sometimes I leave drawings for you in the apartment. They're gone the next time I visit. Sometimes you leave me notes on the kitchen table, telling me when you'll be free next. Your handwriting is printed in block letters, pragmatic, bold, as forthright as you are. Sometimes we spend a business morning or a Saturday afternoon in the apartment. Sometimes we take walks together. You're always planning new walks, showing me cityscapes you'd like me to draw. You have a good eye; I might also say a quirky eye. At first, I think that eye is clinical. Dissecting the world for its financial value. What will sell? What can a strategist pick out of the visual clutter to include in a high-end, marketable portfolio? But more and more, I think you may have a secret artist in you. A slice of white bread on a muddy river, soggy and beginning to sink before the gulls can reach it. Rusty girders under a bridge. The rust looks like paint streaking down from the iron rivets. A dandelion garden surrounded by a black metal railing. Fruit in wooden boxes. Shrimp on stained ice. Playground with sunlight. Lamppost with horizontal car-swipe scratches. Macy's bag stuck in a sewer grate. That last picture has an auditory component because of the way the bag crinkles in the wind, but I can't capture sound in my sketch. Workmen around a hole in the street, looking down into it as if they've discovered a subterranean evil. Mounted police. Pigeon. Wood chip on the corner of a stone fountain. Candy wrapper.

Your left big toe. As we sit on a low concrete wall, your shoe off to give your foot a rest, I draw your toe. An erotic experience, you call it. I don't ask what you do with the drawings. I never ask what you do on the in-between days. I presume you have other lives to live. A curtain hangs over those other lives like one of those artfully folded drapes in the background of an oil portrait. I like the drape. I like the way it accentuates the principal figure in the portrait. I like the way it draws my eyes to the you as you are in my presence, and I have no desire to lift it up and look behind it. That last thought is not quite honest. I have something more like an agitated desire to look behind the drape and know who you really are. I'm developing a fascination for you. But I'm also fascinated by the experience of not knowing. I'm seduced by the hankering. To know the truth about you would ruin the hankering. It might ruin your aesthetic essence. Sometimes, however, you inch up the drape on your own and show me more than I need to know. For example: We're sitting on opposite sides of the little table in your kitchen, talking over dinner, sharing turkey chunks out of the same Styrofoam container. You love to talk. You talk and eat. You seem to have an urgency to get in every action possible. You stab your food with a white plastic fork, tuck a piece of it in the back corner of your jaw, and talk around it. *I'm buying you a new jacket.* You waggle your fork at me. *It's almost winter and you can't keep warm in that thing. Tell me what kind of jacket you want – I'm shopping for gloves tomorrow. Men's gloves. That's what my husband wants for his birthday – black suede gloves. I love the way suede smells when it's new, don't you? So winter. So Christmas. Then it goes raggedy in no time. I'd never buy it for myself, but . . . he likes it. Anyway, tell me what you want – I'll buy you a nice jacket.* You pick up your plastic cup of sink water and drink deeply, your eyes on me, curious and friendly and unashamed. It's the first time you've ever mentioned a husband to me, and it's no accidental slip, but I don't believe it's a calculated goad either. The topic came up and you spoke your mind. Now you're curious what my reaction will be. The word "husband" sends a sickening shock through me. It's not that I assumed you were unmarried. I didn't assume anything. I didn't have a clear idea about it. I didn't want to. I liked the mystery. Now, the takeout food is suddenly a tasteless mush and I'm officially an accessory to adultery. How old-fashioned and yet still surprisingly potent a realization! A weak, five-o'clock sunlight falls through the apartment window over the sink and makes a skewed pattern on the tabletop. None of the angles in that shadow pattern are square. Everyone's moral compass is pointing a different direction and we're all so damn self-certain. It's blind luck if we find someone with the same concept of love. But city people are adaptable. They've made a game out of romantic misalignment. They've turned it into an addictive thrill, this business of violating each other's expectations. The moment of sickening horror when you come face to face with an incompatible morality, isn't that half the allure of the hookup culture? I suppose it must be. Affairs, secret trysts, open relationships, alternative lifestyles, experiments, friends with benefits, polyamory, dyadic, triadic, quad, swinging. Infinite love, I've heard hookup culture called – an idealist's phrase.

Metropolitan roulette – that's another phrase I've heard, referring, I suppose, to the risk of disease, though the risk of emotional trauma is probably greater. Supposedly we're all connected by seven degrees of sex, a vast structure covering the globe like a gigantic doily that Aunt Agatha knitted. Me, I know little about the world of casual, hyperconnected love except through hearsay. I've always kept myself apart, always watched from the edge. How did you macramé me to the global doily? You have a confidence, a charisma about you. That's how. But my dinner is still tasteless. I put my fork down and run my fingers over the worn-out material of my jacket. ~~I generally like denim. Green denim.~~ <u>*I figured. I'll find you something good in denim.*</u> Look at us. Here we are, two ordinary people talking about suede and denim, and yet consider how much has passed between us. You know that I know that you know. We're spending more days and more nights and more dinners and more long, rambling conversations and something is happening to us. We're growing dependent on each other. What began as a business transaction, and then a curio affair, is starting to get into our internal organs and bother us. When you're not sitting on my park bench next to me, I find drawing difficult. The graphite is hard to put on the paper. It turns into grit. It annoys me. I actually give up midway through one woman's portrait. I hand her a nose, an upper lip, an eye, one of my more successful efforts. *That's like a weird Picasso thing, isn't it?* She coos and giggles. *Can you draw another eye under the mouth?* All right, I indulge her and draw an eye under the mouth. Then give her the drawing for free because I can't stand the sight of it or the sound of her idiot giggle. I'm done. The portraitist's pout. I'm customerless and listless and tired. Terribly, terribly tired. And yet also terribly agitated. The agitation doesn't always show. I'm hunched and still as if an early winter has already frozen me to the seat. We're in an orange October, dried oak and maple leaves on the ground, muddy paths turning to a chilled rubbery clay. The first cold spell has struck. Reality bites my skin as I sit on my bench and I'm shivering, my hands pulled up into my new denim sleeves. I can't draw in this temperature, even if a customer does come by. My fingers are too sluggish for artistic nuance. Fifty degrees, forty degrees, I can pretend that my style has a rugged idiosyncrasy, but around thirty-eight degrees, I can't pretend anymore. My finger joints don't work properly. I know the sound of your feet in the dead leaves. You stop and stand in front of me, seeing me now for what I am, no longer that locally famous park icon, just a shivering homeless man hunched on the frosted seat of a bench, without any use in this world, frozen mucus encrusting the cuffs of his new jacket where he's wiped his nose, a dead leaf clinging to his hair, a pencil pathetically still clutched in his hand. What can I do? It's the reality of winter. I've survived it many times before. If I could spruce up for you, I would, but I can do no more right now than huddle with my collar turned up over my ears. Well, I suppose I could pull the leaf out of my hair, but what's the point? The homeless and the CEO. When you finally find your voice in a gush of steam from your lungs, you blurt out, _Starving Artist, this is getting ridiculous._ Lately, I've become obsessed by your choice of words. What exactly is the "this" that is ridiculous? The cold? My thin, raggedy appearance? Our relationship? My trouble cranking out the art-house drawings that interest you enough keep you bound to me? I know I'm in a bitter mood. Part of that mood is seasonal discomfort, but most of it comes from how tightly wound up I am inside, wanting you and at the same time resenting how much I need you. That feeling makes me unforgiving toward the both of us. I sit in an obstinate silence and look at the ground, until you finally blurt out what's in your heart. _This was never supposed to be a relationship. It shouldn't be costing me so much emotional trouble._ ~~Everything's a relationship. What else are we going to call it? If I draw a rock, I have a relationship with the rock. If I draw a tree, I have a relationship with the tree.~~ I'm feeling petulant enough to be nasty. Right away you flare up. _So I'm another art project? I'm just another fucking tree?_ You can't help the bitterness jumping out of your mouth. _I didn't come here to argue. Let's not. Let's really not. I only wanted to make a suggestion._ For a long time, you suggest nothing. You stand and look at me. You seem reluctant to speak, as though you know I won't like it, and suddenly I know what you're going to say. _I want you to move into the apartment._ You're glaring at me and pointing toward Fifth Avenue. _Not just visit now and then. Fucking hell – live there properly, why don't you? Make it your home. At least for the winter. I can give you a little cash every week for groceries and . . . you know . . . better clothes._ You're eyeing my dirty toenails ripping out through the ends of my sneakers. Here we are at our worst, both of us at our most combative, and you still manage an act of generosity. Me, I'm not as evolved as I like to pretend. I'm in such a cynical mood that I'm thinking: So it's to be a corporate takeover? I'll lose myself and my freedom? I get it: The winter is a threat to your new commodity. What if a patrol officer finds me frozen behind a bush like a broccoli? Better to store your art acquisition where you know it'll be safe, under your control. It's always about control with you. (I'm working myself into a rage.) And me? I'm just as despicable. I can be bribed. Isn't that what's going on here? I can be bribed by a handful of cash and by warmth on a cold

October day. I can be bribed by a queen-sized bed in a closet. I can be bribed by a hot shower. I can be bribed by a warm body beside me once a week. Alas for the halcyon days of sleeping on a rock in Central Park, eating breadcrumbs and picking my nose. What's happened to me? What's happened to my private utopia? Even my drawings are your property now. I give them to you and you give them to your high-end art friend, whom I imagine bedecked in black clothes and jingling metal bangles. You're using me, and at the same time flattering your ego by "helping" me. The thought of you finally caging my life makes me so angry, I can barely look at you. I know it's a misplaced anger, but I can't help it. For a long moment I can't say yes. I grit my teeth, squeeze my fist so hard that I break the pencil and a splinter of wood pricks the skin of my palm. The pain takes me out of the moment, and I relax and capitulate. All right. I accept. I'll bow to the pragmatics of the season and take up residence in the Dali apartment. Just for the winter, mind you. In the spring, I'll emerge and earn my own independent living again. Ho ho, but see how independent the park artist is now. I'm a latchkey boy. Over days and weeks, I let myself in and out. After a while I don't even bother letting myself out. I linger inside. I barely use the money you give me. I'm an expert at living on next to nothing, and I still have a stash of my own bills in the plastic sandwich bag in my jeans pocket. Your twenties, crisp out of a bank machine, pile up on the windowsill untouched. After a few weeks, something aesthetically strange happens to them, and I think it's because I'm spending too much time in isolation. The stack of cash begins to develop a personality. It channels your spirit. The bills take on the fascination of having been inside the pocket of your blazer and in your hands. They have a trace of your skin oil on them, maybe even a trace of your smell. The pile accumulates like a plant growing in the weak sunlight on the kitchen windowsill, a little lopsided. Sometimes I talk to it. When you visit, I'm prone to confusion, because I can't remember which ongoing thread of conversation I'm having with you and which one I'm having with your totem. The apartment is becoming a private society. I talk to Dali. I talk to the money stack. I talk to the radiator. As could have been predicted, I start to draw on the wall. I can't help it. The ugly yellow wallpaper grates on me more than usual one day, when I'm feeling removed from the rest of the world. The color is like a drug trip. I don't even know what I'm doing until I notice a pencil in my hand and a sketch taking shape. I can't say what it is. I ask your totem: What are these lines? Why am I drawing them, Totem? They don't make a face. They don't make a skyline. They're scribbles as freeform as my thoughts, and I let them unfold and ruin the wall. I'm sorry, Totem, for ruining your wall. But not sorry, really. I don't mind it, if you don't. The trail of the pencil is like a trail of piss to mark my territory. I wuz here. I am here. I live here. I belong here. The next time you enter, you don't even comment. Your eyes rove over the scribble, your voice pauses a beat, and then you take a quick breath and continue to talk fast and earnestly about a new walk you'd like to try with me along the Hudson. New walks, new vistas, new scenes you'd like me to draw. I can't keep up with your energy.

You are relentlessly externally oriented, and I'm perpetually internally focused. I try, but I can't keep up. How many drawings have I given you so far? What are they worth? Who is your art contact, this curator of a private gallery? Will I unwittingly walk into that gallery someday and find my own drawings leering back at me with price tags on them? How much money are you making off of them? Why do you admire that sketch of the vengeful pigeon attacking a person? Who is the pigeon to you? Who is the person? How much do you bench-press at the gym to get that kind of upper arm definition? How often do you chew the finger-nails on your left hand to get them so ragged that they feel like emery boards on my back? Why do you love the bitterest coffee? How can you despise vanilla ice cream – who does that? – and yet love Twinkies? Why do you hate pota-toes? Not just politely dislike them in a stew, but angrily hate the sight and smell of them? Why do you speak so damn fast? Why do you roll your eyes in annoyance? Why do you walk so quickly down the street? Why are you so of-ten amused and so often annoyed, and why do you switch so quickly from one to the other? Why is your moral compass so self-certain? How many Manhattan apartments do you own, with a boyfriend installed in each one? What makes you come back to me every week or so? Why do you snore? And you do. Not loudly. A steady, quiet, polite snore that lasts until you turn over. I don't know how to draw a snore, but I wish I could. Maybe the scribble on the kitchen wall is a drawing of your snore. Or maybe it's a seismograph of my own agitation. Jaggedness rising. You glance at it from time to time, monitoring it as it grows over the wallpaper. How can you stand me and how can I stand you? That's the question that eats at me. It's a philosophical conundrum worthy of late-night pillow talk. *How can you stand me when I'm so phlegmatic?* I am, too. I'm now spending my days rolling around your apartment, daydreaming in the radiator warmth, mulling the outside world in my imagination – which is to say, keeping the world at an infinite distance. I live off cheap food and rusty-tasting tap water. I hardly ever draw anymore. But if you're disappointed in your acquired artist, you don't show it. Instead, you answer me with your own question. *How can you stand me when I'm so polyandrous?* You do cut to the chase. I'm in a mental confusion, trying to justify my tolerance toward your infidelity. See how deftly you've turned what might be considered your fault into mine? ~~*Five points for the fancy word. All right. We both know that polyandry is the proper state of the modern woman. Why should I want anything less than an exemplary modern woman?*~~ Your hand flops onto my stomach in a languid gesture, both dismissive and affectionate, as we lie side by side. *Is that really your rationalization?* ~~*It's not a rationalization. It's true.*~~ *That's what you tell yourself? That you like me having other men?* ~~*It did make me uncomfortable, but now I'm okay with it. And, yes, I admire it.*~~ *You're flattering me. Do I get more flattery points if I juggle more men? Can I cash in the points for a reward?* In a swift gesture, claiming your reward as it seems, you roll on top of me and our moment of talk is over. But the question does linger. It's in my mind as we have sex. Watching the expression on your face, which is as intense as if you're straining to defecate, I'm thinking, why do we work so well together? Why do the parts fit? If we have no relationship and no promise and no stability and no future, if you're elite and I'm dregs, if you're outward-looking and I'm inward-looking, if you're an extroverted main-sequence star radiating energy to the outside world and I'm an introverted black hole sucking energy and compressing it into my psychological core, if six days a week you're living other lives with other people, if I'll go back to my park bench and my drawing as soon as the spring weather returns and, like as not, never see you again – if our connection is so fragile – then why am I so deeply moved by certain moments that we have together? I know the answer. It's precisely because of the fragility of the relationship. Sometimes, when I look at you, I think I almost understand the loveliness and fragility of all experience. You illuminate the truth to me. So I admit it – I've turned you into an art object. Well, well, I get what I want out of you, just like you get what you want out of me. We humans can be selfish and generous at the same time. After sex, we lie next to each other, catching our breaths, slippery with sweat in the overheated coffin, staring up at the ceiling. And then you do something unexpected. You do it only once in all the many times we've been together. Do you remember? You start to cry. I've never seen you cry before. I'm surprised that such a thing is physically possible. You? Self-certain, muscularly and intellectually and economically strong modern woman, you, the one who seized what you wanted and so started the whole affair between us? I don't even know what that oozing water is at first. Why are you sweating out of the corners of your eyes? Oops, it's tears. And now, a moment later, the sound of sobbing comes out of your throat, a sudden, bitter sound, scrubbed of all weakness. My hair prickles. My stomach curdles. You mutter ferociously, _Don't try to comfort me. OK? Just let me cry._ The predicament lasts three minutes and then you're done and you give me a friendly pat on the leg. Was that your own reaction to the fragility of life? Did we share the same thought at the same moment and react each in our own way? I know better than to ask. It'll only spark an angry retort. Anger is your song. And it fascinates me, is what

I'm saying. I'm surrendering to you. I'm having trouble seeing anything else, any other object, any other person or cityscape or street or pattern of sunlight, except to understand how *you* might see it. I'm beginning to see through your eyes, feel through your skin, smell through those slightly asymmetrical nostrils of yours. I don't need to sit in the park and draw. I don't need to take walks through the city and spy out the scenes that you want me to sketch. I don't have the energy anyway. I don't need my eye's micrometer anymore. I want *your* vision. I want to hear your own description of the bare tree on that particular corner that looks like it's trying to flag down a taxi because of the way a branch sticks into the street. I'd rather stay in the dim hush of your apartment and wait for you and hear you and absorb your experiences and draw what I think you've seen, like a grub in a chrysalis waiting for his wings to come back after a flight around the meadow. Or like a blind bard learning about the world by proxy. Honestly, if I don't need my eyes anymore, why don't I just poke them out? As an offering to you, I mean. A medieval devotion. A self-mortification. My thoughts are getting progressively weirder in the isolation. How love can scramble the brain! Or maybe I'm just sleeping too much and losing my sanity. I could offer my eyeballs to you in a plastic beer cup. As to how to get them out of their current situation – a sharpened pencil might be apropos. A gesture of surrender, it seems to me at the moment. Like a man whose will is broken might cut off his testicles and give them to his captor, so I might cut out my eyeballs and hand them to you. I'm leaning over the sink in your bathroom, examining my face in the mirror. My eyes, empty almond shapes, stare back. Didn't I say an artist needs to put his blood on the page? I could dip my finger in a bleeding eye socket and draw your face on the bathroom mirror. I could certainly draw you blind. I'm an expert on the shape of your face. That's when you come home, kicking off your shoes and rattling your keys onto the kitchen table. You look around the open bathroom door in curiosity. *Honestly, do you have to sharpen that pencil in my sink? You'll clog the drain. I'm deciding how to poke out my eyes.* I study my face in the mirror, turning my head side to side. You don't respond. Not in words. You stand contemplating me with a half-grimace, half-smile, a strand of black hair tracking across your cheek and stuck in the corner of your mouth. I think you fathom the moment. You seem to weigh just how much of the moment is a humorless joke, how much is performance art, how much is my own rambling, troubled internal conversation – what might happen and what probably won't.

Chapter 5

A week later, apropos of nothing, at two in the afternoon as you're sitting at the foot of the bed pulling on a knee-length, black leather boot, you look over your shoulder and say, _Are we really in so much pain that you're about to enucleate yourself? Are we really there?_ Our conversations always unfold over long stretches of time with gaps in between. I lift my head off the pillow to examine your face in profile, then lie flat again. You always surprise me with the range of your vocabulary. Enucleation – removal of eyes. You don't seem to be making light of the topic. You look more ill than anything. You look strained. You look tired. Damn, I've been self-absorbed. I should have been taking better care of you, or taking any kind of care of you at all. If I knew more about your other lives, I might know how to help, or at least I might appreciate the complicated mix of stressors that brings you down at the moment. I suppose the grinding burden of management, the responsibility of millions of corporate dollars passing through your hands, the logistics of a personal life full of too many secret compartments including the one that you share with me – that would be enough to wear a person down. You turn back to the difficulty of squeezing your foot into the boot without rubbing off the Band-Aid on your heel. _Can you come to lunch today? I want to show you something._ These days I rarely emerge, but I accept the invitation. Something tight in your voice suggests that you're going to show me more than a new vista that you want me to draw. We meet a friend of yours for a late lunch at a corner restaurant, in Battery Park, near the river. Your friend is already seated at one of the outdoor tables. Dumpy, middle-aged dude in a pumpkin-colored sweater that clashes horribly with his ginger hair. Is _this_ the famous art curator? He's most definitely not the skinny, elderly person with punk hair, nose ring, bangles, and black clothes that I expected. You've never shown me any part of your external life before, and I get the feeling you're about to tear a blindfold off my eyes. The middle of December has treated us to an unexpected flood of sunshine, a warm day, a last opportunity before the sidewalk tables are locked away in storage. We greet your friend and sit. The black iron tabletop is painfully cold to the touch. The conversation is yours and his. I listen. I watch. The less I say, the better. I'm here as bric-a-brac, as a part of the New York décor. I'm the crazed, starving park artist, remember? My rags look even more ragged under the new denim jacket. In the first minute, I realize that he's not an art curator. He's your husband. I know because he's wearing black suede gloves that he pulls off and tucks into his back pocket before he eats. He doesn't seem to notice me and certainly doesn't register that you and I are together in any manner more than passing acquaintances. To be fair, he's so besotted by you that he may have no brain capacity left to process me at all. Why did you bring me? Do you want me to pass aesthetic judgment on him? Or is it your way of breaking up with me? Or breaking up with him? Or pouring gasoline on your life and setting it all on fire? Or maybe, less cataclysmically, you want me to watch and finally learn about you. All right, I'll sit here quietly and observe while the two of you talk. I nibble a salad and the vinegar turns my stomach. This is what I glean. You're not technically a financial titan. Not in the strictest sense of the word, at least. Not a business tycoon, highflyer, jet-setter, wheeler, dealer, mover, or shaker. Instead, you work part time, inspecting cardboard insect traps in office buildings. Some of the highest-caliber offices, to be sure. You've gotten on your hands and knees and peered behind the file cabinets of some of the richest people in the world. As for a jet-set lifestyle, you haven't been to an airport in a decade, and you haven't left the city in even longer except for a daytrip once to the Jersey shore in plastic sunglasses and ten-dollar flip-flops. You're a middle-class nobody with a soppy husband whose devotion to you is nauseating and endearing. He's just as overpowered by you as I am. Two sops staring at a lady. I detect, implicit in his indulgent good humor toward you, a faint, disturbing whiff of condescension, as if he sees you as a twelve-year-old girl and not as a woman with a will of her own. And he doesn't curate art, either. Dude owns a local store. He curates specialty potatoes and yams. No track-lit corner with a display of my sketches. Only unpainted wooden bins of tubers. I can smell the dried soil just by thinking about it. He loves to hear you talk as you eat your cheese sandwich and flash your teeth at each bite. He wants to know about your art club, the self-improvement hobby that has occupied your time over the past five months. He's proud of you for discovering a passion and a new group of friends, even if he has to write you a check every week for the tuition. Yes, this is the truth of your financial acumen – you figured out how to embezzle two-figure checks from your husband. Every week, you leave home and attend the Park Bench Art Retreat, which buses its eager group of students to a variety of picked locations along the Eastern seaboard to provide for a diversity of views and visual experiences. You should be its spokesperson. You sound like a brochure. Did he remember to bring your portfolio from the hall closet? He lifts the black case from beneath the table. He loves the sketches you bring home. He finds them amazing, really, given that you started half a year ago. With an expression on his face between pride and parental indulgence, he clicks open the case and thumbs through the sheets of drawings with his broad grocer's fingers. The vengeful pigeon is a favorite of his. And whose toe is that? Is it your own toe? And look at that sketch of a tree flagging down a taxi. You're good at trees. Not so good at faces. They come out strange. Not quite human. A little weird. A little spooky. Actually, a little like a yam. But you'll get the hang of it. All it takes is practice. When do they let you graduate from sketching to painting? A cold breeze ruffles the papers, and he closes the case with great care and pushes it across the table to you. He must assume I'm one of your classmates. His eyes pass over my chair briefly while he stoppers up his mouth with a burger. It's weird that he doesn't acknowledge me, doesn't even ask me what my name is.

When you smile at him, the flashing of your teeth brings out the skull in your face. It's a smile of suppressed fear. You've brought us together with no prior explanation and you're letting the drama play out. You love this potato dude, don't you? You hate him and need him. I can see the emotion in your face, the way you eat, the way you sit. You despise him for being dumb enough to trust you, while at the same time you admire him for his – his what? His kindness to you? You feel superior and self-loathingly inferior. And you must hate the subtle, parental way that he owns you without even knowing that he's doing it. You know I could expose you. I could ruin your marriage in five words, like spilling a bowl of hot soup in his lap. He'd jump up with a yelp of pain. You're daring me to do it, aren't you? Leaning back in your chair with your long black coat unbuttoned, you look like you've slit yourself open to show me your guts, all your coiled lies. But one lie in particular takes me by surprise for its audacity – the lie about your mother's apartment. Turns out she passed away a year ago, and I'm sorry to hear about your loss. I am. She seems to have been your anchor. As Potato puts it, too bad you had to let go of her apartment. That terribly ugly condo just off Central Park, with the yellow décor and the garish fake painting. Remember that crazy dump? Still, it was a valuable piece of Manhattan property. Could have been fixed up, new kitchen, new wallpaper, rented out, would have supplemented the store income by a good twenty-three and a half percent. Who knows what New York yahoo got hold of it when the estate was settled. Well, well. Can't be helped now. He always said you should have let him oversee the estate, but of course you had to be stubborn and handle it yourself. He shrugs his pudgy shoulders and sighs in gastric contentment. He does a thorough wipe of his mouth with his napkin as if cleaning up a spill on a store countertop, then stands, takes his suede gloves out of his back pocket and draws them on, gives you a peck on the lips. The warmth is leaching out of the sky. You remind him that you'll be home late tomorrow. He wishes you a wonderful, productive time at the art retreat and walks away, his shambling gait exuding a well-fed, puppyish trust. On balance, I like him. I feel warm toward him, as if he were an actual potato cooked perfectly and mooshed up into a nice, soothing consistency with butter. When he's gone around the corner, you look at me, your skullish teeth on display in something horribly between a grin and a fearful grimace. You've destroyed yourself. You've been lying to me for the past five months about who you are. We leave the restaurant and walk for a while without speaking, because what is there to say? You toss a pebble over the wall of Battery Park and it disappears in the black water. The gesture is bitter, an expression of revulsion, like spitting a bad taste out of your mouth. The sun has just gone down and the cold of winter is descending on the evening. We lean together on the low wall at the water's edge, looking out across the river. A December evening has just fallen, post lunch, pre dinner, the sky is dark, windows shine out from across the water and cast long, colored, eel-like streaks in the ripples. I had better say something because the silence between us is stretching and maybe you're worried that I'll erupt in a fit of rage. I could snatch the brief-case of drawings from your hand – my draw-ings! – and whap you in the head with it. I can already hear the hollow sound of that whap. Or I could fish the brass key out of my pocket, throw it at you in disgust, and stomp away. Im-agine all the rage I could justify. But that kind of emotion isn't in me right now. I feel empty, like you've pulled my insides out. I don't know if I can talk to you about what I've just learned, at least not right here, right now, in the open, while people are walking behind us and my un-derstanding of the world is trembling in so much confusion. I want to go back to the apart-ment and talk in private. I want to ask – who are you? I thought I was the artist, but all these months, it's you, you're the one, you've been painting a full-color portrait of yourself, of you as you wanted me to see you, and now you've flipped it around to show me the back. You're telling me, look, look at the coarse weave on the canvas, look at the dirty wood frame, look at the rusty staples, look at the flyspecks, that's who I am. And all I can think to say is, ~~Um, when do you leave for Japan?~~ You turn and squint at me in incredulity. _Sorry? What?_ ~~_Aren't you meeting with the Nippon group all week?_~~ You emit a bitter gasp of laughter. _Oh, Starving Artist. Is that how it is? All right then, I fly out tomorrow. What do you want to do in the meantime?_ ~~_Do you want to get an early dinner? I didn't eat very much at lunch._~~ You nod, looking down into the lapping water, and then blurt out another gasp of laughter. _Good idea._ As we walk away, you hug yourself in the cold air, then link arms with me and put your head against my shoulder. For the moment, you have me and I have you. Except we don't. We don't have each other. Too much has been left unsaid, expanding between us, pushing us apart, so that even though you're pressed against me, I feel as if you're walking on the other side of the street. There's another truth for you to tell me. I dread it, but I want to know, I want to ask, and I'm afraid of it. I'm afraid of something much worse than confrontation, something I don't even know how to name. We walk and we find a low-grade pizza parlor and share an early dinner, a single large plate of spaghetti and meatballs. We always eat cheap together. Come to think, for such a corporate high-roller, how come you're always eating crap food out of plastic plates? How did I never notice it before? I don't like the Parmesan, so you sprinkle it on your side of the meal. We don't talk much. When we're done, we stand up and cram the plastic dish into the top of a garbage bin. Now we're walking uptown to the Dali apartment. We could take the subway, but the night is clear, if a little cold, and walking is a welcome distraction. The city at night is an astonishing kinetic clutter. The darkness and brightness trick the eye. Everything looks far away and close at the same time. The noise is distant and unrelated until suddenly a bus booms in our ears and then rushes behind us and is distant again. I don't want the walk to end, but it does, and now I'm sitting on the foot of the bed, waiting, watching you, while you sit at the little round kitchen table with a pad and a pencil, sketching me. *Go ahead,* I say, *tell me the rest.* I know what it is, of course, before you speak. *I'm sorry,* you say, as you sketch. *I keep looking at my life and thinking: But I'm Achilles, Slayer of Men, remember? Business tycoon? That's who I'm supposed to be! I'm important! Not this . . . whatever it is . . . weak . . . nothing person . . . under the thumb of him and him and him. But at least I have an apartment that nobody else knows about. And I can fill it up with my imagination. That's why I made you up. I know, I'm a fabulist. Is that so bad? I've been dining off the latest fantasy for months. Me and you. Do you know what I mean? But now . . . You're falling apart on me. I can't hold you together anymore. If only it were as simple as a break-up. Is it stupid that I feel bad for you? I feel bad that you're unraveling. I can't stop it, because fantasies only work for a while, and then they don't, and then they die. Just like everything else in the world. If I could exert a supreme effort of will, like deistic creation, and keep you knitted together, make you real, hold you with me, that's what I'd do, but it's no good, it's all breaking up and sloughing off and draining away and I can't stop it. You're unsustainable. Do you hear me? Unsustainable! And now? Now I'm back to nothing again. Nothing. I'm sitting here alone, at a little round table, in a little Manhattan apartment, talking to myself, and even my made-up park portraitist is gone. He's flittered away like butterfly wings.*

Portraits:

An Experiment in Skill Learning

In 2007, when I was 40 years old, I decided to learn how to draw portraits in pencil. I had always doodled, as far back as I could remember, but was never a portraitist or a proper artist. As a scientist, I decided to do an experiment on the effect of practice. I planned to draw 1,000 portraits and then assess where my skill level lay. Hypothesis 1: Through repetition, it's possible to learn to draw in a manner that looks like talent. Hypothesis 2 (the null hypothesis): After 1,000 tries, I'll still be embarrassingly bad.

I bought a bunch of sketchbooks and pencils, put up photos of people's faces on my computer, and drew them, sometimes quickly over about 10 minutes, sometimes carefully over a few hours. At first, the drawings were horrible, but over three years, they improved. The excruciatingly slow hand-eye learning was fascinating to me. By the mid- to late 200s, the drawings looked skillful. Number 224, for example, is in a different universe than number 17. I stopped at 450, because, by that point, I considered the experiment over and Hypothesis 1 to be verified. I haven't drawn portraits since, and I suspect my skill has degenerated, maybe almost back to baseline.

After all that drawing, my brain was a little obsessed with pencil portraiture. I would see it, and feel it, and smell it, as I was lying in bed going to sleep at night. And that mind space was the origin of the novella *Love*. The book is obsessed with drawing specifically portraits in pencil. The main character obsesses over it and sells his drawings for 5 bucks a piece in Central Park. The story is about him using words to draw portraits of himself and the woman that he meets — and in the end, about the woman having spent her time drawing portraits in her imagination of herself and of him. It's all inspired by pencil portraiture.

Here I'm including a selection of 24 drawings spanning the learning process from absolutely terrible – no discernable talent – to double-take level of skill by the end. I don't feel egotistical in praising the final drawings of the series because I can't draw like that anymore. It's beyond me.

The experiment has a philosophical significance to me. There is a self-serving tendency for people to view talent as an inborn property. If it's inborn, then I have an excuse for not having it. Those people are lucky, and I am not, at least in that particular respect. That view absolves me of any accusation of laziness. My morality, my personality, my self-worth are left unchallenged. But I always half-suspected that talent equals attentive practice over time.

$$\text{Talent} = \text{Attention} \times \text{Practice} \times \text{Time}$$

The concept is similar to Gladwell's 10,000-hour rule to become an expert. I'm not sure I'd subscribe to an exact number, however. I also think that rote practice is not effective compared to focused, attentive practice. Attention is the key. And focusing attention over many hours requires motivation. And motivation is a complex emotional state that depends on internal makeup and external support. So maybe there is a role for inborn talent after all, but maybe that role is different from the way it's usually conceived. Maybe a talented artist has a special kind of emotional and motivational structure on the inside, which allows for sufficient bursts of hyper-focused attention on a task. Maybe Da Vinci was never born as a visual, hand-eye genius but instead born, and raised, and supported by others around him to have a specific kind of motivation structure.

Of course, given the same amount of attention, time, and practice, some people will improve faster or reach a higher level. Let's allow for some variance across the population. What I'm suggesting is that anyone, or almost anyone, who can apply enough *oomph* to the task over enough time will become very, very, impressively good. One might say this person is better than that person, as one might argue that Mozart is better than Schumann, but they're all nonetheless excellent.

This perspective is both depressing and encouraging. Depressing because it means that every person with a talent is proof of my own personal laziness. I can't excuse myself anymore by saying, "I never did have the talent for painting. Or for languages. Or for sports. Or for juggling. Or for this or that or the other." One is forced to confront one's moral limitations. But at the same time, it's encouraging because it means that within broad limits, most people have extraordinary potential.

In any case, the only way I could think to test the idea was to take up drawing portraits, since I was so obviously bad at it and had been so for 40 years; practice it with the most focused attention I could muster; and then see whether skill did or did not emerge. It emerged. I consider the primary hypothesis to be confirmed.

Michael S. A. Graziano
Princeton, NJ
2026

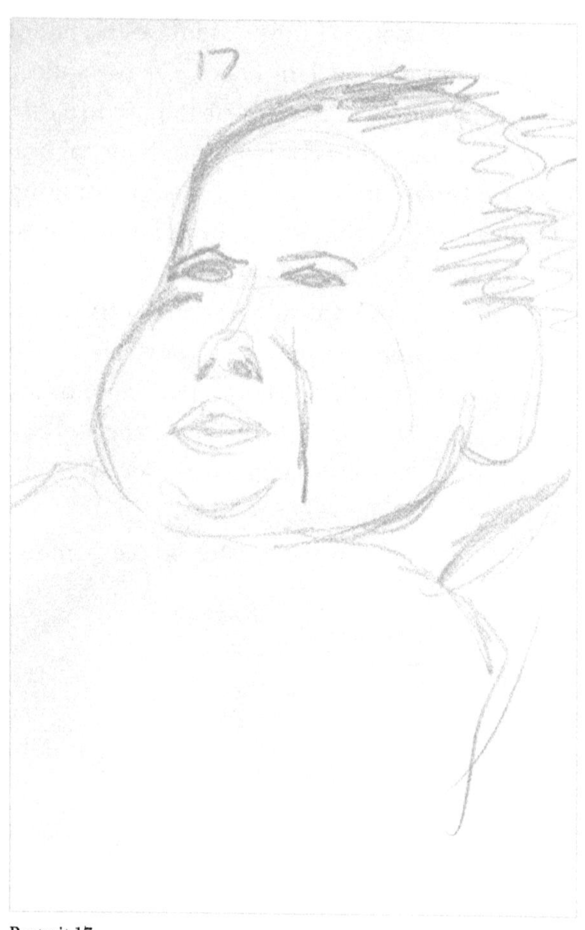

Portrait 17

Portrait 92

Portrait 107

Portrait 120

Portrait 134

Portrait 145

Portrait 170

Portrait 172

Portrait 193

Portrait 200

Portrait 202

Portrait 204

Portrait 206

Portrait 223

Portrait 224

Portrait 246

Portrait 251

Portrait 255

Portrait 258

Portrait 264

Portrait 266

Portrait 267

Portrait 276

Portrait 425

About the Author

Michael S. A. Graziano, PhD, is a professor of neuroscience and psychology at Princeton University. *Love* is his latest work of fiction published by Leapfrog. Others include *The Love Song of Monkey*, *The Divine Farce*, and *Death My Own Way*. He has also published popular science books including *God Soul Mind Brain* (Leapfrog Press, 2010), *Consciousness and the Social Brain* (Oxford University Press, 2013), *Rethinking Consciousness* (W. W. Norton, 2021), which was a finalist for the Penn-Faulkner award, and most recently, *Charlie's Lab* (Press 53, 2023). He has regularly written for *The Atlantic*, *The New York Times*, *The Wall Street Journal*, and other media outlets. He lives in Princeton, New Jersey, with his wife and a backyard fox family.